THE CHRISTMAS SNOWSHOES

Amish Romance

HANNAH MILLER

Copyright © 2022 by Tica House Publishing LLC

All rights reserved.

No part of this book may be reproduced in any form or by any electronic or mechanical means, including information storage and retrieval systems, without written permission from the author, except for the use of brief quotations in a book review.

Personal Word from the Author

To My Dear Readers,

How exciting that you have chosen one of my books to read. Thank you! I am proud to now be part of the team of writers at Tica House Publishing who work joyfully to bring you stories of hope, faith, courage, and love.

Please feel free to contact me as I love to hear from my readers. I would like to personally invite you to sign up for updates and to become part of our **Exclusive Reader Club** —it's completely Free to join! Hope to see you there!

With love,

Hannah Miller

VISIT HERE to Join our Reader's Club and to Receive Tica House Updates:

https://amish.subscribemenow.com/

Contents

Personal Word from the Author	1
Chapter 1	4
Chapter 2	10
Chapter 3	21
Chapter 4	30
Chapter 5	40
Chapter 6	50
Chapter 7	60
Chapter 8	66
Chapter 9	81
Chapter 10	90
Continue Reading...	103
Thank you for Reading	106
More Amish Romance from Hannah Miller	107
About the Author	109

Chapter One

Nicole Lantz clutched the stack of books tightly, puffing as she made her way over to one of the reading tables at the back of the library. She put them down with a thump and fell into a nearby chair, rubbing her stiff arms and looking eagerly at the book on the top: *Little House on the Prairie*.

"Think you've got enough books?" joked a sweet voice from the other side of the table.

Nicole smiled. "It's winter. There's not as much to do right now."

Viviana Holt smiled, brushing back a lock of her glossy black hair. Nicole glanced away, running a hand over the soft white *kapp* on her own head, making sure her hair was still neatly covered. Even after all this time, it still seemed odd to be talking to someone whose hair flowed freely over her shoulders.

"Well, I can't wait for Christmas break," Viviana said, looking back down at the textbook open in front of her. She tossed down her pen and sighed, stretching elaborately. "I'm pretty sick of studying."

"You're almost done though, right?" said Nicole.

"Almost. One more exam, and then I'm free." Viviana chuckled.

"I pity you." Nicole shook her head, smiling. "I was more than ready to be done with school when I was fourteen."

"Well, so was I, honestly, but you know what parents are like." Viviana shrugged. "They insisted on college, even though I was pretty happy to just get to work right away as a barista."

Nicole didn't know what that was, but she knew exactly what parents were like – in fact, hers already disapproved of her friendship with Viviana. She didn't know what to say, so she reached for her first book instead, cracking it open. "Don't you ever read for pleasure anymore?"

"No. Doesn't seem to be much point to it when I have to read so much for studying." Viviana nodded at the stack of books again. "I'm starting to think maybe I should run away and join the Amish, too, so I can spend my days reading and doing… like, farm stuff."

Nicole laughed. "Winter is nice, and a much-needed break after all the harvesting. I'm looking forward to curling up in front of the warming stove with one of these. Of course, things get a bit busier around Christmas, but we still have a few weeks to go."

"I loved playing outside on Christmas break as a kid."

"Me too. These days, I have so many chores outside that it doesn't seem like fun to be outside in the winter." Nicole grinned. "But I loved snowball fights with my brother. Still do, sometimes."

"My brother's pretty cool, too. We didn't have a lot of snowball fights, though. Mostly, we went snowshoeing."

Nicole cocked her head to one side, intrigued. "Snowshoeing?"

"Yeah. You know, when you put snowshoes on and walk around on the deep snow."

Nicole glanced out the nearest window. While the library was snug and cozy, with its deep carpets, rows of books and the electric heater humming in the corner, the view through the window was white and cold. Icicles dangled from the eaves of the library, sparkling in the afternoon sunshine. The lawn beyond was a carpet of snow.

"I've never heard of it," she confessed.

"Oh, but it's so much fun." Viviana laughed. "The snowshoes feel funny on your feet, but once you get the hang of walking in them, it's pretty cool to walk around on deep snow that you'd normally sink into."

"How do they work?" Nicole asked.

"It's simple. They're just like normal shoes but with really wide soles, so it spreads your bodyweight around, keeps you from going through the crust of the snow." Viviana grinned. "You've *got* to try it, Nicky."

No one else ever called her Nicky, but she found that she liked it. She smiled, holding up her book. "Well, I'll put it on the... what did you call it? That list of things you want to do before you die?"

"Bucket list," said Viviana.

"I'll put it on the bucket list," Nicole joked, knowing full well she didn't have one. It would be silly for an Amish woman to have one, wouldn't it? The rest of her life would consist of marriage, children, and homemaking, whether she liked it or not. She'd even found the husband already... well, prospective husband, in any case.

"Snowshoeing is *not* bucket-list-worthy," snorted Viviana. "It's something you've just got to try, with friends. Hey – why don't we go home and try it out now? I'm not getting any studying done anyway, my brain is too full. But there's some really deep snow in our backyard, and I've got a pair of snowshoes that'll work for you."

Nicole yearned to go with her. Viviana was so sweet and fun, and such good company, but she knew her parents already didn't like the thought of them spending time together at the library. What would they say about going to Viviana's house? It would be full of *Englischers*.

"Sorry, Viviana. I don't think that's a good idea," she said.

Viviana looked crestfallen. "You always say that when I ask you to hang out outside of the library. Come on, Nicky. Aren't we friends?"

"We are," said Nicole quickly, upset by the sorrow in Viviana's eyes. "We definitely are. I just… well…" She sighed. "I have to be here at five for my father to pick me up and take me home. I don't think there's enough time."

"Oh, of course there is. My house is only five minutes away by car. We can pop over there, do some snowshoeing, and be back by four if you want."

Nicole rubbed her *kapp* again, uncomfortable. "By car?"

"Yeah. I mean, it's not a problem, is it?" said Viviana. "I've seen Amish people getting out of taxis and buses all the time."

"Well, it's not forbidden to ride in a car," said Nicole slowly. "We're not allowed to own a car. Or drive it. But…"

"So, what's stopping you?" Viviana slammed her book shut and jumped to her feet, grabbing her car keys. "Let's go."

Nicole glanced over her shoulder at the frosty world outside again. *Mamm* and *Daed* wouldn't be happy about this, she knew. But Viviana was right: there was nothing in the *Ordnung* against riding in a car. In fact, her neighbor's son often got a ride to town with his *Englisch* friends who lived across the road from them. And her parents had never commented on that, had they?

She bit her lip, then looked up at Viviana's excited, sparkling eyes, and told herself it would be rude and wrong to turn down her friend's invitation.

"Okay," she said. "Let's go."

"Yes." Viviana grinned, punching the air. "Come on, Nicky. You're going to love it. I promise."

Nicole hefted the books in her arms and followed Viviana to the door. The books were heavy, but the guilt growing in her heart was heavier.

Chapter Two

Viviana's car zipped through the streets at a breathtaking speed. Nicole clutched the handle by the window, watching in amazement as blocks flashed by in a matter of minutes. Viviana was right: in just five minutes, they were pulling up in front of a pretty house in the suburbs, surrounded by a lawn that was buried in snow. Pine trees rose up on either side of the house, which was decked out with all the trappings of *Englisch* life: satellite discs on the roof, wires running this way and that, the blue flicker of a television screen in the window.

Even though it was still a few weeks before Christmas, the home was already gaudily decorated. Strings of lights hung in bright, neon colors from the windows and doorways; there was a gigantic inflatable snowman on the front lawn, plus a huge Christmas tree glimmered in the window.

Viviana jumped out of the car. "C'mon, Nicky. This way," she said. "Don't mind Mom and Dad – they're in the sitting room, watching reruns of some reality show as usual. Just wave at them when we go past."

It was so strange to think Viviana wouldn't want to introduce Nicole to her parents right away. She waved obediently as they walked around the outside of the house, but the two older *Englisch* people were sitting on the couch staring at the screen and seemed oblivious to Nicole's existence.

"I think Chad's home, too," said Viviana, leading Nicole around to the backyard. She tugged at the door of a garden shed. "Probably playing video games, so he won't bother us. Ugh. This thing is stuck."

"Here," said Nicole. She gave the shed door a solid tug, and it flew open.

"Wow, girl," said Viviana. "You're pretty strong. Anyway – here they are."

Viviana reached inside and pulled out two of the strangest shoes Nicole had ever seen. They consisted of large oval frames, webbed with what looked like nylon straps, and were quite light in Nicole's hands when she lifted them.

"See? This distributes your weight. Makes it possible to walk on thick snow," said Viviana. "Let me strap them on for you."

Nicole sat down on the porch steps and Viviana knelt in front of her, strapping the snowshoes on over Nicole's plain boots. "Why don't your boots have laces?" Viviana asked.

"I don't know. It's the style we use," said Nicole shyly.

"Are snowshoes allowed?" Viviana asked, her tone a little derisive.

Nicole swallowed. "I don't know."

Viviana looked up, hesitating. "Hey, you know, I don't want to make you do anything that goes against your principles or anything."

Nicole stared down at the snowshoes on her feet, then squared her shoulders. A great wave of longing to do something new washed over her. "*Nee.* I want to try this."

"Okay. Cool." Viviana got up, brushing soft, powdery snow from the front of her jeans. "Here – let me give you a hand up. They're going to feel really weird for the first few minutes."

Nicole took Viviana's hands and got to her feet. Her balance wobbled, and she took a step to correct herself, stepping directly onto the inside edge of one snowshoe. She squealed, clutching Viviana's hands.

Viviana giggled. "It's okay. I've got you."

Panting, Nicole looked up at her friend, happy excitement rushing through her. "How do I stop myself from falling over?"

"Take these." Viviana grabbed a pair of poles with snow baskets from where they leaned against the shed. "They'll help you to keep your balance."

Nicole took them, digging them into the snow on either side of her, and carefully moved her feet left and right. Steam curled around her face as she breathed.

"There," said Viviana. "Easy, right? Now, when you move, just swing your feet wide so that you don't step on your snowshoes."

Nicole nodded determinedly and took a firm grip on each of the poles. Slowly and carefully, she took a shuffling step forward. The snowshoes felt surprisingly heavy on her feet, and after just a few steps, her hips began to ache from widening her stance. But she couldn't stop the smile spreading over her face. It had been so long since she'd last done something completely new.

"You're doing great," laughed Viviana. "Now go more toward the lawn – the snow's much deeper there."

Nicole shuffled further into the backyard. Her poles were digging deeply into the snow, and when she stepped out onto the pristine white surface, she expected her feet to sink in. But they barely sank down at all.

"Look at this," she squealed with delight, taking a few more steps. "I'm not sinking." She laughed, the sound bursting easily from her lips.

"You go, girl," Viviana cheered.

Laughing, stumbling, clutching her poles, Nicole staggered around on the snow. In a few minutes, she was walking almost easily, amazed at how deeply her poles were sinking into the snow when she was almost walking on the surface. There were only a few inches of snow here, but she could imagine striding over snowdrifts almost as though they were solid ground.

"That's it," Viviana called.

Nicole couldn't remember when last she'd had so much fun. Dizzy and breathless, she stamped this way and that, giggling. It was a whole new world of fun and adventure for her.

"Watch out," Viviana shouted suddenly. "There's a patch of ice –"

It was too late. The pole in Nicole's left hand struck the patch of dark ice a split second before she saw it. The pole skidded helplessly, with Nicole's full weight resting on it, and she stumbled, trying to catch herself. The front of one snowshoe caught on the back of the other, and Nicole's belly lurched as she fell –

A strong arm was flung around her chest, and Nicole found herself being boosted back onto her feet.

"You all right, there?" rumbled a masculine voice.

Startled, Nicole looked up into a pair of soft brown eyes much like Viviana's. They widened when they rested on hers, and a smile burst across the broad, friendly face, which sported dark blonde stubble.

"Oh – I'm sorry," she gabbled, pulling back.

The young *Englisch* man grinned at her, keeping a hand on her shoulder. "Got your balance back?"

"*Jah - jah*, I do, thank you," stammered Nicole. She stepped back and almost fell again; the *Englischer* grabbed her arm to stop her from tipping over.

"Sorry to startle you, Nicky," said Viviana with a laugh, crunching through the snow beside the man. "This is my brother, Chad."

Nicole had heard a lot about Chad from Viviana. He was two years older than she, at twenty-two, and worked at a mechanic shop in town. Nicole managed a faint smile. "Nice to meet you."

"Nice to meet you, too." Chad laughed. "Having fun, are you?"

"*Jah*," Nicole confessed. "I haven't enjoyed something this much in years."

"Well, I used to suppose you people don't have a whole lot to enjoy," said Chad cheerfully. His eyes sparkled. "But judging by the looks of you, there's plenty of fun where you come from."

Nicole felt her cheeks heating, even more so because of how conscious she was that his eyes really were very dark, and his smile really was very beautiful. She dropped her gaze to the snow, reminding herself she already had Hamish. Besides, Chad was *Englisch*. Even looking at him would land her in terrible trouble with her parents.

Her parents. She turned to Viviana. "What time is it?"

"Oh, it's half past three already." Viviana blinked, surprised. "Time sure flies when you're having fun."

"It does," said Nicole. She gave Chad another nervous glance, then returned her gaze to Viviana. "This has been wonderful – truly. Thank you so much. I just have to get back to the library now."

"Yeah, I need to get ready for my shift at the restaurant, too." Viviana checked her phone.

"I could take Nicole back to the library if you're busy, Viv," said Chad. "I know you've still got to get ready."

"Aw, would you?" asked Viviana. "That'd be great. Do you mind, Nicole?"

Nicole glanced nervously at Chad, but she didn't want to inconvenience Viviana. Besides, the library was close by. She managed a hesitant smile, trying not to think about what Hamish would say if he knew she was taking a ride in an *Englischer's* car – with a man, no less.

"No, I don't mind," she said.

"Wonderful." Viviana gave Nicole a quick hug, then mock punched her brother in the arm. "Thanks, bro. You're the best. For now."

"For now," snorted Chad. He shook his head, his eyes filled with tenderness for his little sister, then turned to Nicole. "Okay – let's get you out of those snowshoes."

"Oh, yeah." Viviana turned to Nicole. "Before I forget... I want you to keep the snowshoes."

"You – you do?" Nicole gasped. She looked down at the shoes, then up at Viviana, her heart flipping over. "Oh, Viviana, I couldn't."

"You've got to," said Viviana simply. "I've never seen you have so much fun before."

Nicole didn't want to say that she couldn't remember when last she'd had so much fun. She stared down at the shoes again. What would her parents think? Well, they didn't run on electricity, so she supposed they wouldn't be forbidden.

"But they're yours," she hedged.

"I can't remember when last we even wore them. Definitely not since Dad broke his ankle three years ago." Viviana laughed. "It's better for you to have them. You'll enjoy them."

"Oh, Viviana, thank you." Nicole felt a burst of excitement at the thought of walking the fields in these snowshoes this winter instead of slopping through the deep snow to break ice on water troughs or rescue trapped animals. "Thank you so much."

She hugged her friend again, and then Viviana hurried off. Nicole unstrapped herself from the snowshoes before Chad could help her. He took them from her, shaking the snow off them.

"To the library, right?" he asked, leading her around the house to where his truck stood beside Viviana's car in the driveway.

"Yes, please," said Nicole.

"Cool." Chad held the passenger door for her. "Ladies first."

Nicole felt a blush rising to her cheeks despite herself. She scrambled up into the seat, and Chad got in beside her, and the truck's engine was quickly roaring. He leaned back to look through the back window, putting a big hand on the headrest right beside Nicole to do so. He was very close, and she felt a moment's panic before he turned forward again and put both hands on the wheel to head down the street.

"So you're Amish, huh?" he said. "I'm sure you don't bring a lot of business to my boss's mechanic shop."

Nicole couldn't help laughing. "Well, we do have buggy makers."

"Buggy makers. Pretty crazy. I never even thought of that." Chad laughed. "Is it true that you guys really don't have phones?"

"We don't," said Nicole. "Telephone shanties, though, for emergencies."

"I guess it's better that way," said Chad unexpectedly. "I mean, we all just spend half our time scrolling around meaninglessly." He gestured at the Christmas decorations shining on the streetlights as they left the suburbs behind and headed toward the library. "So, do you guys have Christmas?"

"Of course, we do." Nicole smiled. "It's the birth of Jesus. One of our favorite and most festive times of the year."

Chad glanced over at her, returning her smile. "That's pretty interesting. I bet you cut your Christmas trees right there on the farm."

"No, we don't have trees." Nicole smiled. "We don't really do the decorations, except for candles, cards, and maybe some greens."

"Keeping the Christ in Christmas, right?" said Chad jovially, and Nicole began to like him a little better at once. But it was too late to say anything more. He was already stopping the truck in the library's parking lot, and Nicole climbed out, pulling her coat close against the biting wind.

"Hey, Nicole," Chad said suddenly.

She looked over at him. His eyes were unreadable. "I'll see you around sometime, right?" he said.

"I'm sure you will," said Nicole.

Chad nodded, then burst into a grin. "Don't forget your snowshoes." He held them out to her.

Nicole grabbed them with a smile, then watched as Chad drove away, the lights from the library windows reflecting brightly in the smoothly polished surface of the truck.

Chapter Three

The buggy arrived at the library half an hour later, while Nicole was reading the first of the books she'd left stashed with the librarian when she'd gone to Viviana's house. She was sitting at the same table she'd shared with Viviana earlier when the chime of harness bells from outside caught her attention. Looking through the window, Nicole saw her parents' buggy driving toward her, the fine tinkle of the bells filling the air. The sunshine had given way quickly to clouds, and fat white flakes were drifting gently down, settling like stars on the black coat of the buggy horse. *Mamm* and *Daed* sat in the front seat, bundled up in their coats, the buggy's canvas roof pulled up against the snow.

Gathering her books and tucking her new snowshoes under her arm, Nicole waved goodbye to the librarian and headed out into the snow as the buggy moved slowly forward in the parking lot. It came to a halt beside her, and *Daed* gave her an impatient glance. "Come on, Nicole. We need to get back to the farm before it storms."

Nicole placed her books into the backseat and carefully laid her snowshoes on top of them, reaching up to scramble into the seat. "I'm in," she said.

Daed gave her a long look from under his hat, then glanced at the snowshoes. "What are those?"

"Snowshoes, *Daedi*. Aren't they *wunderlich*?" Nicole held one of them up. "You strap them onto your shoes to walk around in deep snow, and – "

"I know what snowshoes are, Nicole," said *Daed*. "I wanted to know where you got them."

Mamm laid a hand on his shoulder. "Then you should have asked that, *liebchen*," she said calmly.

Daed ran a hand over his face. "You're right. I'm sorry. It's been... a tough trip."

"Why?" asked Nicole. "What's wrong, *Daedi*?"

"It's the weather forecast," said *Mamm*. "Apparently, we're in for a very stormy winter. Your *vadder* is worried for the sheep."

Nicole could understand his fears. She remembered when she was a young girl, there had been a bitterly cold winter, and they had lost many of the lambs. That had been a hard, hungry year.

"I'm sorry," she said softly. She held up the snowshoes. "I'm sure we could use these, then. They'd be so useful for walking in the fields and trying to find the sheep."

"I didn't give you money to buy toys like that, Nicole," said *Daed* tightly.

"I didn't buy them," Nicole said quickly.

Mamm turned to look at her, raising her eyebrows. "Where did you get them, then?"

"Well…" Nicole paused. "My friend Viviana gave them to me."

"The *Englischer*?" snapped *Daed*.

"*Jah*." Nicole lowered her eyes. "I didn't think they were against the *Ordnung*, and she was so sweet about them, and I thought they could be useful, and – "

"They're not against the *Ordnung*, *dochtah*." *Daed* turned the buggy around and chirped at the horse, which broke into a brisk trot. "I just don't want you accepting gifts from *Englischers*. We are a people set apart – you know that."

"I know, *Daed*." Nicole bit her lip. "They were only a gift. They don't mean anything."

"I hope not," said *Daed* quietly. "Our hearts can be so easily led astray. But don't let the *Englisch* fool you. Many have good hearts, but they're not the same as we are. Never forget that."

The horse trotted toward home, and Nicole sagged down in the backseat, her heart heavy. The snowshoes lay over her lap, and she ran her hand over them. All the fun she had had with them just a few minutes ago seemed to have dissolved now. As always, it had ended in disappointment for Nicole.

She clutched them tightly. She was going to find a way to have a little fun and adventure in her life, no matter how hard *Mamm* and *Daed* tried to stop her. They seemed to think she wanted to become *Englisch*, which she never would. She just wanted to try some new things.

"Well, you have a nice weekend to look forward to, don't you, *dochtah*?" *Mamm* asked encouragingly. She smiled back at her, clearly trying to cheer you up. "Didn't you say Hamish was going to take you for a buggy ride tomorrow?"

"He is," said Nicole, smiling as well as she could. "I'm looking forward to it."

But the words were not completely true.

Nicole was on her hands and knees, reaching for the furthermost egg in the nesting box. A hen clucked angrily right beside her ear.

"Can you stop that?" she hissed.

The hen clucked all the louder, alarmed. Nicole ignored her, reaching past until the smooth shape of the egg slipped into her fingers, then sat back out of the chicken coop. She added the egg to the small basket beside her. Out of their ten hens, only three had laid today. Winter had its troubles. At least *Mamm* had water glassed many of the eggs from summer.

As she straightened, the rumble of an approaching buggy caught her attention. Nicole turned, dutifully putting on her best smile as a plain bay horse trotted into the yard, drawing a buggy that gleamed with polish. The harness, too, shone in the sun; its buckles caught the last of the evening light with dazzling brightness. Bells jingled on the harness as the horse came to a halt in the yard.

"Evening, Nicole." The buggy driver raised a hand in greeting. He was sturdily built, his shoulders tight against his neat black suit, and there was a faint smile on his clean shaven face.

"Evening, Hamish. I'll be right there." Nicole turned and hurried up the steps of the porch, but before she reached the front door, it opened. *Mamm* quickly took the egg basket from her.

"What are you doing? You don't keep a man waiting," *Mamm* said sharply. "Especially not when he's courting you."

"*Jah, Mammi. Danke.*" Nicole smoothed down the front of her skirt and glanced at her reflection in the front window, straightening the strings of her *kapp*.

Mamm helped her, tugging on one of them. "I don't mean to snap," she said softly, "but you know Hamish Bontrager is an excellent match for you."

"*Jah, Mamm*," said Nicole obediently. "I'll see you a bit later."

"See you later. I'll keep dinner warm. Remember to invite Hamish in if he wants some," *Mamm* added.

Nicole hurried down the steps and up to the buggy, smiling. "Sorry to keep you waiting."

"It's all right," said Hamish graciously. He reached under his feet as she climbed up beside him. "Here you are." He was holding out a thick driving blanket, soft cotton on the bottom, sturdy corduroy on top.

"*Ach, danke*. That makes it much more comfortable." Nicole spread the blanket gratefully over her lap.

Hamish inclined his head, saying nothing, and turned the horse and buggy around. He clicked his tongue and the horse set off down the lane at a brisk trot. Nicole leaned back, stealing a glance at Hamish as he drove. His eyes were fixed on the road; he had fine, high cheekbones and very blue eyes, as though he had stepped straight out of Switzerland himself, instead of his ancestors so many years ago.

The bells jingled merrily, and the countryside was perfect. It shimmered under a blanket of white snow. Bare-limbed trees and post-and-rail fences were etched against the snow like charcoal drawings on white paper. Little barns slumbered under coverings of snow, and here and there a copse of trees looked like something from a story, the trees all dusted with white.

It was beautiful, and Nicole knew she was being ungrateful. Still, it chafed at her that Hamish had hardly said a word, even though they had been driving around the farms for several minutes already. Shifting her weight, she broke the silence.

"Have you ever worn snowshoes?" she asked him.

Hamish frowned across at her. "Snowshoes?"

"*Jah.* They're these big platforms that you strap to your feet. It makes it easier to –"

"I know what snowshoes are," said Hamish impatiently. "I've seen *Englischers* wear them at times." The way he said "*Englischers*" made it sound like a curse.

"They're not against the *Ordnung*, though," said Nicole. "And I... well, I got a pair. As a gift."

"A gift?" Hamish raised his eyebrows. "From who?"

She started to wish she'd chosen any topic of conversation except for this one. "A friend." She cleared her throat. "Viviana."

"The *Englisch maidel* from the library?" Hamish's frown deepened. "Why is an *Englischer* giving you gifts?"

"Because she's a *gut* friend, Hamish." Nicole didn't want to argue with him. "Besides, I think they're very practical. They'll be so useful for walking around the fields, if we get the big snow they're forecasting for this Christmas."

"I suppose." Hamish shook his head. "Why are you so taken with this Viviana in any case? You have plenty of Amish friends. You should spend time with them instead."

Nicole stared down at the blanket warming her lap, feeling suddenly very alone. Had no one else ever felt restless? Had no one else ever wondered if there was more to life than simply doing as one was told?

"Viviana is *gut* and kind," she said softly. "You'd know that if you ever met her yourself."

A lump stood out in Hamish's jaw as he gritted his teeth. "Well, maybe I should."

"Should what?"

"Meet her myself."

Nicole looked up at him in surprise. "Why, Hamish, I've invited you with me to the library so many times, and you've never wanted to come before."

"Well, I'm not as busy now, am I? Christmastime is more peaceful for me." He gave her a thin smile. "I can come with you, next time you go. Then I could meet this Viviana that you're so taken with."

"*Ach,* Hamish, that would be *wunderlich*." Nicole clapped her hands. "You'll love her, I know you will. And you'll like the library, too. There's a huge section on organic farming, and even some Amish authors, too."

"Maybe," Hamish grunted. "At any rate, it'll be *gut* to meet this *Englischer*."

Nicole smiled, hoping he was finally showing some real interest in something she liked. And she knew that if he met Viviana, he would be able to tell that she was a good person... and *Mamm* and *Daed* would take his word for it.

She settled back in her seat, smoothing down the blanket. Maybe Hamish would be the one to convince her parents that her early Christmas present was worth keeping.

Chapter Four

Nicole wiped her palms on her skirt. Hamish was holding the library door for her, and he glanced at her swiftly as she stepped through it. "What's wrong?" he asked.

"Nothing," Nicole said quickly, smiling. "Why would something be wrong?"

"I don't know. You just seem – nervous." Hamish frowned.

Nicole widened her smile. "Not at all. I guess I'm just excited for you to meet Viviana. Then you'll see how nice she really is." *And you'll realize that not all* Englisch *people are as bad as you think*, she added silently. If she'd said that aloud, Hamish would have wanted to go straight home, so she didn't.

The librarian waved cheerfully to Nicole as they walked past the front desk, giving Hamish a knowing grin and Nicole a little wink. Nicole could feel her cheeks warming as she led Hamish toward the back table where she always sat. It still felt so strange to her that *Englischers* openly acknowledged courting couples. But maybe it was better that way. Maybe courting was something to be openly celebrated, not kept so secret.

She chided herself mentally, dragging her thoughts away as they rounded the shelves. Viviana was sitting at the table, flipping open her laptop and arranging her college books, and to Nicole's shock, Chad sat right beside her. She couldn't help but notice the way his tight black sweater sat over the strong lines of his shoulders and collarbones. He was looking around the library as though bored, and he didn't have any books with him.

"Who's that?" Hamish growled in her ear.

"Um, Viviana's *brudder*. Chad," she whispered back.

"You didn't tell me about *him*," said Hamish angrily.

Then Viviana looked up, her black hair tumbling back from her face in a shining curtain, and her wide smile flashed in the library. "Nicky," she sang out. "Oh, you brought a friend."

"Hi, Viviana." Nicole glanced nervously at Chad, who was looking up at her, a smile spreading across his face. "This is Hamish."

"Well, hi, Hamish." Viviana got up and extended a hand, her smile dazzling.

Hamish, to Nicole's surprise, reached out and gripped Viviana's manicured hand in a handshake that lasted a few seconds longer than what she thought necessary. She had never seen him shake hands with a woman before.

"It's nice to meet you, Viviana," he said, his voice deep and warm. Nicole hadn't heard him speak English since the eighth grade, but he was more fluent than she'd expected.

"It's nice to meet you, too." Viviana's cheeks were faintly pink as she let go of his hand.

"Hey, Nicole," said Chad, dragging Nicole's attention away from the other two. He flashed her a smile and put a foot on the chair opposite him, pushing it out for her.

"Hello." Nicole sat, arranging her skirts neatly. "Are you studying today, too?"

"Oh, he *insisted* on coming." Viviana laughed as she and Hamish sat down opposite each other. "I've never seen my brother so interested in books before." She gave him a playful elbow to the shoulder.

Chad's cheeks reddened slightly, but he kept his eyes on Nicole. She didn't know what to say, and looked down at her lap instead, wishing she'd thought to pick out a few books before coming to sit here. Hamish was dead silent beside her. She felt her toes curl inside her simple boots. This was unbearably awkward.

"So." Viviana cleared her throat. "What do you guys have planned for Christmas?"

To Nicole's surprise, Hamish responded at once. "Well, the schoolchildren have been working on their Christmas program for weeks. It's going to be a great one."

Viviana cocked her head slightly to one side, allowing a wing of hair to fall over her shoulder. "Christmas program?"

Hamish smiled. "It's like a school play, except everything depicts the birth of Christ. Normally, there are shepherds, angels, even a little Nativity scene."

Nicole laughed, feeling her stomach unclench slightly. "Do you remember the year that the Hochstetler kids brought a real live donkey to the program?"

"I do." Hamish grinned; a real, genuine smile, the likes of which Nicole hadn't seen on his face in a long time. "And it almost bucked Mary off."

Viviana laughed merrily, cupping her chin in one hand. "I did a Christmas play when I was a kid, too. I was one of the angels, but my halo fell off."

"Sounds about right," quipped Chad, and they both laughed. Even Hamish laughed. Nicole stared at him.

She dragged her eyes away, telling herself not to be foolish. "So, Viviana, why do you decorate Christmas trees?"

"Gosh, I hardly know." Viviana shrugged. "It's just a fun tradition to us."

"Yeah, but let's be real." Chad grinned. "Gifts are the most fun Christmas tradition."

"Definitely." Viviana turned to Hamish. "Do you guys give gifts at Christmastime, too?"

Nicole chipped in before she could stop herself. "Oh, *jah*. We love to give small gifts as symbols of the Wise Men giving gifts to Jesus, and also to spread joy and celebrate His birth."

"What kind of gifts?" Chad asked, smiling at Nicole.

"Normally practical things," said Nicole. "Last year my mom sewed me a new *kapp*." She tugged at her headpiece. "And my brother, Mark, made me beautiful new handles for my dresser."

"My parents gave me a new bridle for my buggy horse." Hamish turned to Viviana. "What about you?"

"Oh, all sorts of stuff. Clothes, beauty products, that sort of thing." Viviana grinned over at Chad. "And my brother saved for months to buy me these nice new earphones I wanted. He's a softie, actually, just don't tell anyone."

"Hey," Chad growled, but he looked pleased, and Nicole couldn't help smiling at him. The glance he gave Viviana was filled with obvious love.

The conversation flowed easily after that, and it was all too soon that Nicole glanced out of the window and saw that the light was already growing low. She and Hamish took their leave slowly, and it was only when they reached the buggy that Nicole noticed she'd forgotten to check out any books.

Hamish's eyes were shining as he got into the buggy, taking the reins. Before Nicole could say anything, he looked over at her, grinning.

"Goodness. I had no idea *Englischers* could be like that."

"Like what?" Nicole asked.

He clicked his tongue, sending the horse out of the library parking area. "Like… like us," he said slowly.

Nicole smiled. "I knew you'd like them if you met them yourself."

"Well, I do." Hamish laughed. "Viviana is so smart. She's such an interesting person."

Nicole wrapped her driving blanket more tightly over her lap. This was exactly what she had wanted, she thought, listening as Hamish went on and on about Viviana. So why did she feel so discontent now?

∽

Nicole smiled over at Hamish as he stopped the buggy at the farm's gate. "*Danke* for taking me," she said, interrupting him as he was telling her about how interesting *Englisch* Christmas traditions were.

"Oh – of course," said Hamish vaguely.

Nicole managed a smile, wishing she'd never brought him to the library in the first place. "All right."

"See you tomorrow."

"*Jah*." Nicole got down from the buggy, and Hamish turned it around sharply and drove off down the lane. He didn't glance back to see her wave.

Sighing, she wrapped her arms around herself against the biting wind, snowflakes swirling around her. Maybe they were right about this December being harsher than usual. Hearing voices from the barn, she avoided the house and went over to the old red building, pulling open the vast doors and stepping into the hay-scented warmth.

Two young men looked up as she came in. They were crouched in the far end of the barn, where her father kept the implements, a scattering of planks lying around them as they worked on a wooden frame about hip-height.

"*Gut* afternoon, Mark, Stephen," Nicole called out.

Her brother, Mark, had a handful of nails in his mouth. He nodded to her, waving briefly with his hammer, and mumbled around them. "Hi, *shvestah*."

"Hello." Mark's best friend, Stephen Byler, gave her a shy smile. He was a tall, slender young man with a shock of blond hair that almost fell into his soft brown eyes. "Find some *gut* books?"

"Not today." Nicole sighed. She wished she'd paid attention and gotten some books. Now, she had a long, quiet Saturday afternoon to look forward to, with no company and little to do. "What are you guys doing?"

"Building a manger for the Christmas program." Mark laughed. "Stephen's *groossdaedi* volunteered him."

"I guess there are disadvantages to living with your grandparents, especially if one of them is a deacon." Nicole smiled at him.

Stephen shrugged, his cheeks turning faintly pink. "I don't mind. I'm just glad Mark was happy to help."

"Anytime." Mark grinned. "Were you looking for *Mamm* and *Daed*?"

"*Nee*," sighed Nicole. She didn't want to face their questions about how things had gone with Hamish. "I wanted to help, actually. Can I do something?"

Mark spat the nails out into his hand. "You can hold these."

"Gross, Mark." Stephen took the nails, laughing, and offered Nicole a can of clean ones. "You could hold *these*."

"*Danke.*" Nicole grinned, feeling some of the tight knots in her heart untie themselves as she took the can.

"*Danke* to you." Stephen took a fresh grip of the wooden frame. "Is it aligned now, Mark?"

"*Jah*, it's *gut*." Mark held out a hand. "Nail, please."

Nicole passed him one, and he began to hammer it in place.

"Are you coming to the Christmas program?" Stephen asked her over the noise.

She pulled up an empty bucket, turned it over, and sat down. "*Jah*, of course. I wouldn't miss it. Sarah is playing one of the angels."

"I wouldn't miss it, either." Stephen smiled but dropped his eyes to his hands again. "I'm sure it's going to be fun."

"I'm looking forward to the Christmas youth dinner most of all," said Mark. "It's about time we had one again."

"*Jah*. It's going to be *gut*." Stephen grinned.

"It better be." Mark laughed and held out his hand for another nail. "Your *groossdaedi* got you onto the planning committee, didn't he?"

Nicole handed Mark the nail. "Well, Hamish and I are on it, too," she said. Her stomach knotted again at the thought of the next committee meeting, which would take place tomorrow. Hamish had promised to drive her there. She wondered if he would spend the whole drive extolling Viviana's many virtues again.

"*Jah*, well." Stephen shrugged. "I'm sure we'll all work together to make a *wunderlich* evening out of it."

"I don't know how you find time for everything," said Nicole to Stephen. "You're caring for your grandparents and also seem to be part of everything that happens in this community."

"Like you said." Stephen chuckled. "*Groossdaedi* is a deacon. He insists sometimes. But I don't mind. I like to be busy." His eyes lingered on her a moment longer before dropping to his boots. "Besides, it's an honor to help the community."

"And your *groossdaedi* has been a *gut* deacon. I just worry about him sometimes," said Mark.

"*Jah*, his health isn't what it used to be. But don't tell him that. I've tried." Stephen laughed. "It doesn't go down well."

"I s'pose." Nicole leaned back against the wall, smiling. She wished that today in the library had been as fun and easy as this was, but she kept thinking back to the way Chad had stared at her.

It was flattering, and it made her blush. But that didn't mean she was entirely sure she had liked it.

Chapter Five

❦

The next day offered a welcome break in the cold, snowy weather. Balmy sunshine poured down over Nicole's shoulders from a sky so pale blue it was nearly white. She readjusted the driving blanket over her lap, raising her face to enjoy the warmth on her skin. The wind was still piercing, but it was good to see the sun, to watch the way it sparkled on the icicles that hung in jagged teeth from the fences surrounding them. The soft chime of harness bells filled the air, punctuated by the merry clop of the horse's feet on the newly-plowed road.

She opened her eyes and glanced over at Hamish. He'd been whistling quietly since they left her home, and now she recognized the tune. It was "O Come All Ye Faithful", and there was a piercing, wistful quality to the way he whistled it. She liked it.

"That's beautiful," she said.

"*Danke*." Hamish cleared his throat. "Viviana said it was one of her favorite Christmas carols."

Nicole lowered her gaze to her boots, feeling her toes curl. "I like 'Hark the Herald Angels Sing' best."

"Oh, you do?" said Hamish. He went on whistling, "O Come All Ye Faithful."

Nicole bit her lip, but she didn't know what to say. The silence was still hanging between them when Hamish brought the buggy to a halt outside the school. The small, whitewashed building was already surrounded by buggies, a group of horses turned out and blanketed in the small field beside the school.

"I'll unhitch the horse," grunted Hamish. "You go on inside."

"I can help." Nicole smiled shyly.

He shook his head. "*Nee*, it's all right."

Sighing, Nicole climbed down from the buggy and headed into the schoolhouse. Maybe Hamish was just being chivalrous, allowing her to get in out of the cold. But that wasn't the impression she was getting.

It almost felt like he just plain didn't want her around.

She thought back to the day in summer when he'd first asked her on a buggy drive. It had been a perfect night, crystal clear, the stars shimmering, only the faintest breeze fanning her warm skin after a long evening in the Fishers' barn, singing hymns and visiting with all the youth of her community. Her heart had still been thudding with the powerful rhythm of her favorite hymn when Hamish had walked up to her, his eyes reflecting the light of the gas lamp over the door and asked her out of the blue if he could drive her home. No one had ever asked her that before. Nicole had said yes.

She wished she could get some of that excitement back as she ducked into the schoolhouse. The children's tables and desks had been stacked in a corner, and now there were two long tables running down the center of the room. Behind the teachers' desk, Stephen was shuffling some papers. He looked up as she came in and gave a little wave; she waved shyly back, then headed to the table on the right, where a few other girls were taking their seats.

She sat down between two of her cousins, Mary and Lydia, and glanced around for Hamish. The meeting was about to start when he slipped into the schoolhouse and took his seat at the other table with the young men.

"*Gut* evening, everyone," said Stephen. "*Danke* all for coming."

The meeting began, and Nicole tried to listen attentively as Stephen outlined his plan to break the group up into several smaller committees that would each handle one aspect of the youth dinner. It was methodical, and it seemed like a good idea... But her eyes kept darting from her notes to where

Hamish was sitting among the other men. He was staring at nothing, his hand idle on his pen, not writing anything. Was he thinking of her?

But his eyes never went to her. They stared into the middle distance, like he was thinking of someone else. Nicole could guess who.

She dropped her gaze to the table, feeling her cheeks warm. She was imagining it, surely. Viviana was *Englisch*. Hamish was Amish. It was as simple as that. Besides, neither of them would do that to her… would they? She waited for a pang of jealousy to overwhelm her and felt worried instead when it didn't. This was all wrong. She was supposed to feel jealous, wasn't she? She was supposed to want, more than anything, a life with Hamish… wasn't she?

Mary thumped an elbow into Nicole's side. "Nicole," she hissed.

Nicole looked up. "I – I'm sorry. What did you say?"

Stephen was smiling at her from behind the teacher's desk. "I was asking if you would head up the games committee."

"Oh." Nicole swallowed. "I, uh, I thought you were the head of the games committee."

"I'm on it, but I feel you would be better suited to lead it." Stephen gave her a small smile.

She shrugged. "Sure. I'll do that."

"*Danke.*" Stephen turned away, looking at the men. "Hamish, Elijah, I was wondering if you two would be in charge of the seating."

Mary giggled and leaned a little closer to Nicole. "I think he likes you," she whispered.

"What? Hamish?" Nicole blinked at her.

Mary rolled her eyes. "Obviously we know Hamish likes you, since you two are courting."

"Mary," Nicole hissed.

"Oh, we know it's secret, but news travels fast." Lydia grinned. "Still, why else would Stephen put you on the same committee as he is?"

"Because he's best friends with Mark, of course," Nicole said quietly. "Stephen already has a girl he likes, anyway, and I can promise you he doesn't like me in that way."

"A girl he likes?" Mary shook her head. "Why would you say that?"

"Because he never asks any of the girls at sings to drive with him," said Nicole.

"Stephen has never courted. Ever," said Lydia, with authority. "And I would know."

She probably would. Lydia's family farmed right next to Stephen's.

"That's odd," said Nicole. "I wonder why."

"Me too. He's handsome, loyal, and kind," said Mary.

"He probably just doesn't have the time for it, with all the things his *groossdaedi* makes him do," said Nicole.

"Probably." Lydia sighed. "And I think you're right, Mary, come to think of it. I've always thought Stephen was sort of interested in Samantha."

"Ooh, you're right." Mary tittered. "He *does* like Samantha."

Nicole shook her head, tired of her cousins' gossip. She was relieved when the meeting came to an end, and she could head outside again into a cooling afternoon, the sun slipping lower and taking its winter heat with it.

Hamish was already there, harnessing up the horse. He worked with small, practiced movements, tightening buckles, sliding the collar over the horse's ears.

"Hello, Hamish." Nicole tried to smile. "So you're in charge of the seating."

"*Jah*, I suppose I am." Hamish didn't look at her. "When did you say you wanted to go to the library again?"

"Um…" Nicole's heart sank. She wasn't sure she could sit there and listen to Hamish talking with Viviana for hours again. "Well… I normally go once a week."

"All right." Hamish nodded.

The silence stretched between them, uncomfortable as taut elastic.

"Why?" Nicole asked at last. "Did you want to come with again?"

Hamish shrugged, backing the horse between the shafts. "You can get on in the buggy. I'll take you straight home."

Nicole did as she was told, blinking back sudden tears. How had everything gone so wrong, so quickly?

∽

Hamish dropped her off at the top of the lane, saying he had to get home and help his father with the chores. Shivering in the now-piercing wind, Nicole wrapped her arms around herself and trudged down the lane alone, trying not to feel too angry about it.

Mark was sitting in the kitchen with a hot cup of coffee when she came in, shivering. He took a deep slurp, looking at her over the rim of his mug, and smirked. "What did you do to make Hamish mad?"

"What?" Nicole stared at him. "Why would he be mad?"

Mark held up his hands. "I was just teasing. Are you all right? Your nose is very red."

"I'm frozen stiff." Nicole pulled a chair up in front of the crackling fire.

"I'll make you some coffee. Extra cream and sugar?"

She smiled up at her brother. "*Danke*."

Mark got up, replacing the coffee pot on the gas stove. "Oh, *jah*. A letter came for you this morning. I forgot to give it to you then." He fished it out of a kitchen drawer and held it out to her.

The envelope was plain and ordinary, with messy writing. Nicole took it. "Who could this be?"

"I have no idea," said Mark. "Maybe *Aenti* Mabel?"

"She has better writing than this." Nicole laughed.

The front door flew open, and *Daed* poked his head around it. "Mark. Can you help me with that old cow, please? She's not eating. I think it's ketosis again. We'll need to drench her."

"Sure. I'm coming." Mark put down his cup and grabbed his coat. "Sorry, Nicole. Looks like you're making your own coffee."

"That's all right."

Nicole waited for the door to close behind Mark before tearing the envelope open. Inside, some notepad paper, and a messy scribble that failed to follow the letter format that they'd all learned in school.

Hey Nicole. I got your address from Viv. She looked it up on Google Maps, though I guess you don't know what that is. Anyways, I just wanted to say I had a really nice time hanging out with you the other day. I would have loved to send you a text, but I guess this is the next best thing. Hope to see you again soon. Chad.

Nicole felt her cheeks blazing. She quickly folded the letter and shoved it back into the envelope before *Mamm* could come in. What was Chad thinking, sending her letters like this?

She thought of the way his eyes had rested on her at the library, and her cheeks burned all the more. Wadding up the envelope, she tossed it into the fire and watched the edges curl and blacken as the flames licked around it until all that remained of Chad's note was ashes.

Why did everything have to be so complicated all of a sudden? She gazed at the Christmas cards adorning the mantelpiece, all so carefully handmade, with construction paper and bits of colorful felt. The writing on them was smoothly composed and very different from Chad's scribbled note.

Pushing back her chair, Nicole buttoned up her coat and headed outside. She'd stashed the snowshoes in the barn loft, and she climbed the ladder quickly, grateful that *Daed* and Mark were so caught up in drenching the cow that they didn't seem to notice her come in. Grabbing the snowshoes from their spot, she hurried back down the ladder and out to where the buggy was standing under the overhang.

She opened the back and slipped the snowshoes inside, then slammed it tightly shut. Her heart was pounding unpleasantly in the palms of her hands and her temples. Her hand hovered on the smooth surface of the buggy for a moment, and she gazed out at the fields. The morning's sunshine was gone; clouds were gathering on the horizon, and Nicole could feel snow coming. Tomorrow morning, this yard and those fields would all be slumbering under a fluffy white blanket.

She closed her eyes tightly, squeezing back the tears as she remembered that day in Viviana's backyard. The laughter had made her chest hurt, and she'd loved the adventure as she stumbled around on her snowshoes. But everything had gone wrong since then. Maybe *Mamm* and *Daed* were right. Maybe everything *Englischers* touched was somehow tainted.

She turned and hurried back into the house, blinking away her tears. There would be no more adventure for Nicole Lantz.

Chapter Six

It was almost a relief that Hamish didn't come to the games committee meeting.

Nicole guessed she should be annoyed that no one was driving her to Stephen's and his grandparents' house for the meeting, but for once, it felt good to be walking on her own. It gave her time to think.

She pulled up her coat collar against the biting cold. The air was motionless today, and fat snowflakes drifted down slowly. At least Stephen didn't live far; just four farms away. Her boots crunched on the fresh snow, and she shook the flakes from her arms and shoulders at intervals. Each flake sparkled like a piece of magic. She held out a mittened hand and let a few flakes gather on it, glistening and perfect.

A sigh escaped her. She wished she could think of a way to get out of going to the library next week. She wished she could think of a way to fix everything with Hamish. But how could she fix it when she didn't know what was broken?

The snow had almost stopped when she walked into the Bylers' farmyard. It was one of the oldest Amish farms in the area; an ancient clapboard house propped up a roof that sagged in places, with a barn just a short distance away. A happy, hairy goat watched from a small patch of grass that hadn't yet been covered with snow under a towering oak tree planted by Stephen's ancestors, chewing its cud as she walked over to the farmhouse.

She tapped on the door, and Joan Byler, Stephen's grandmother, threw it open. "Come on in, Nicole," she said, hugging her. Her arms and dress were baked with the heat of the fire, making her hug seem all the more pleasant.

"*Danke*, Joan." Nicole smiled. "The snow's nearly stopped."

"*Gut*. My husband is still on his way home from town. Come on in. They're in the living room."

Joan led Nicole through an aged kitchen and into a small, warm room of a few couches and a display cabinet placed around a leaping fire. There was a quilt and a few plates in the display cabinet, as well as a single, faded yellow ribbon from a quilting competition. Stephen, Mary, and Lydia were sitting on the couches, enjoying hot cocoa.

"That one's yours." Mrs. Byler steered Nicole into a seat and gestured at a steaming mug. "I've made brownies, too. I'll bring them in."

"*Danke, Groossmammi,*" said Stephen. He smiled at Nicole. "*Gut* morning."

"Morning," Nicole murmured, sinking into the chair. It was good to be around such warmth. She sipped her cocoa, which was rich and deliciously sweet.

"Well, we're all here now." Stephen cleared his throat, moving his gaze to Lydia. The fire was warm, causing two red spots to appear in his cheeks. "So, let's talk about some different games we could play. Anyone have an idea?"

Mary and Lydia exchanged a glance and giggled. Nicole shot them both a glare, then turned to Stephen. "How about charades? That's always fun."

"*Jah*, it is." said Mary, snapping out of it. "I like board games, too."

"Board games can work. Especially since we're inside," said Stephen encouragingly. "*Gut* idea, Mary."

Mary blushed. Lydia quickly chipped in. "Do you remember that time at the Yoders' barn-raising that we hummed or whistled songs and people had to guess which ones they were?"

"*Jah*. That was fun." Stephen laughed. "That's a good idea."

Lydia and Mary rattled off a few more ideas, and Stephen nodded, jotting them down on his notepad. Then he turned to Nicole. "Any ideas, Nicole?"

She blinked. It was so strange not to feel invisible that for a moment she forgot what she'd been thinking about. "Um – actually, *jah*, I did think of something. These games all sound *wunderlich*, but maybe to make them fun and more challenging, we could make everything Christmas themed."

"What do you mean?" Lydia asked.

"Well, we could make it so that we have to use Christmas terms or objects for charades." Nicole smiled at the idea. "And to make it really hard, we could say that you have to use Christmas words for Scrabble. And draw Christmas things in Pictionary."

"Oh, I like that." Stephen pointed his pen at her, grinning. "That's clever."

"That'd be fun. We could use only Christmas carols for the song guessing game, too," suggested Mary.

"*Jah*. You *maidels* definitely have a good handle on this," said Stephen, laughing good-naturedly.

They drank more cocoa, and at one point Joan appeared with even more brownies. The fire crackled. Nicole's chair was very comfortable, and she found herself curling up in it, especially after it began to grow cold, and Joan distributed blankets.

A cuckoo clock down the hall struck twice, and Nicole jumped, surprised. "Is it two o' clock already?"

"It is." Stephen looked up in shock. "Well, I'm awfully sorry. Let me ask my *groossmammi* if we have anything for lunch. You must all be starving."

"I've eaten so many brownies, I don't think I could fit lunch in," laughed Lydia.

"Sorry." Nicole got up. "I have to go. I promised Mark I'd help him to paint that manger for the Christmas program this afternoon."

"Me, too." Stephen rose, setting down his mug. "I can drive you home, if you like, since I'm going there anyway."

Nicole glanced outside. The clouds were still very low, and she could feel the temperature dropping even here in front of the fire. For a moment, she wondered what Hamish would say if he saw them together. But what did it matter? She wasn't attracted to Stephen, and besides, Hamish didn't seem to think there was anything wrong with spending hours talking to an *Englisch* girl.

"*Danke*," she said, relieved. "That'll be *wunderlich*."

"Will you two be all right?" Stephen asked the younger girls.

Lydia nodded. "We came with the buggy, and the roads aren't too bad. I'm sure we'll be fine. Our old buggy horse is as good as they get."

"I remember old Rudy." Stephen smiled. "He was a *gut* little horse even when we were *kinner*."

They got up, looking for coats, packing away mugs and plates, folding up blankets. Stephen hurried outside to get his buggy ready.

By the time the girls had tidied up the livery room and said their loving goodbyes to Joan, Stephen was waiting outside, stamping his feet to keep warm and blowing on mittened hands. The low clouds had brought bitter cold with them, and Nicole felt her nose and ears stinging as she stepped outside. She tugged her coat collar up around her chin, smiling gratefully as she clambered into the buggy beside Stephen. "*Danke* for this. I would have hated walking home like this."

"I think you would have made it." Stephen grinned, taking up the reins and clicking his tongue to the horse. "Especially with your snowshoes."

Nicole stared at him as he turned the buggy around and headed down the lane. "How do you know about those?"

"Your *brudder* told me." Stephen nodded. "They're forecasting a big storm before Christmas. I'm sure they'll come in handy."

Nicole felt a knot in her chest unclench itself at his words. At least there was *someone* in the district who didn't feel the snowshoes were some kind of omen of evil. "I thought so, too. That was why I accepted them, even though the girl who gave them to me is…" She hesitated, glancing at Stephen, suddenly loathe to lose his approval. Approval had become rare in her life all of a sudden.

"There's nothing in the *Ordnung* against accepting gifts from *Englischers*," said Stephen smoothly, and Nicole guessed that Mark must have told him about Viviana. "Especially not useful gifts like snowshoes."

She let out a relieved laugh, leaning back against her seat. It was a closed buggy, and unexpectedly cozy. Looking out through the glass windows, the landscape was pretty as it slumbered under the snow, now that she was out of the wind. The sky and land seemed to blend softly together, shades of white and gray in the distance.

"You're the only one who seems to think so," she sighed.

"How so?" Stephen asked.

"Well, my parents and Hamish think I shouldn't have accepted the gift. My parents seem to disapprove of my friendship with Viviana in general, even though she's *gut* and kind." Nicole shrugged. "I guess I just... enjoy talking with someone a little different, once in a while."

She regretted the words as soon as she'd said them, but Stephen didn't react. He smiled, shrugging. "There are *gut Englischers* out there, even if they believe differently than we do. I'm sure Hamish will change his tune once he sees how useful those snowshoes can be."

Nicole shifted uncomfortably. She hadn't meant to let Hamish's name slip, even if, as Lydia said, their relationship really was common knowledge. Clearing her throat, she straightened out her skirt. "Well, I made up my mind to give them back to Viviana, anyway. Just to be safe."

"A pity." Stephen shrugged. "But I can see why you would do that."

"I'm sure Viviana won't be happy." Nicole sighed. "It's difficult trying to keep everyone happy."

Stephen shrugged. "Perhaps that's not your job," he said. "Perhaps your job is to please *Gott*."

Nicole blinked, not just at the words, but at the easy tone in which he delivered them. Stephen clicked his tongue at the horse and snapped the reins as though he hadn't just opened the door to a whole new way of thinking. She stared at him for a few seconds, wondering if that was why he didn't court. He was too busy, not with his grandparents, but with pleasing the only being in his life whose opinion really mattered to him—God.

It was an alluring thought, and Nicole was silent for a few moments before Stephen turned to her with a grin. "I think the games at the youth dinner are going to be *wunderlich* after this meeting. Your Christmas theme idea was *gut*."

"*Danke.*" Nicole laughed. "Now the food, decorations, and seating committees have to do their work. They have far more to plan than we do."

"We'll help," said Stephen comfortably. "I admit that when *Groossdaedi* first said I'd plan the youth dinner, I was a bit worried. But now I'm enjoying it." He gave her an easy, unpretentious smile. "First, though, we need to get that manger finished up for the Christmas program."

"It's going to be beautiful. Do you remember when you had to play Gabriel in that last Christmas program you were a part of?"

"How can I ever forget?" Stephen groaned and laughed in the same breath. "I told Ruth I wasn't good at talking in front of everyone, even if I was in the eighth grade already. I just took one look at that crowd, and that was the end of it."

"I laughed so much that I nearly dropped Annie's *boppli* who was playing Baby Jesus. I was standing in the wings, waiting to hand him to… was it Talitha who was playing Mary that year?"

"It was. She was hilarious when she said, 'Greetings, you who are highly flavored.' Ruth was so mad at her." Stephen groaned. "And Talitha just glared at me. I don't think she ever heard the end of being highly *flavored*."

Nicole burst out laughing, Stephen easily joining in. It seemed to come so effortlessly to him. She couldn't help feeling a little pang of envy.

"Anyway. Here we are." Stephen brought the buggy to a halt, and Nicole glanced outside to see that somehow, they were already in the yard. The short ride had flown by so quickly.

"*Gut* luck with the manger," said Nicole, her hand on the door. She looked up at Stephen with a smile, feeling a sudden rush of butterflies in her stomach.

"*Danke*." Stephen grinned. "I'll need it."

She looked into his soft eyes for a moment, then quickly opened the door and rushed outside without looking back. If she looked back, she might realize how much she had enjoyed the ride.

Chapter Seven

❦

Nicole reached into the laundry basket, pulling out a damp sheet. The sky was clear enough today, even though the wind snatched at the sheet, making it snap and billow as she wrestled it onto the line. The dampness stung her fingers with cold. She grabbed a last corner and pinned it onto the line with a wooden peg, then stepped back, breathless. Washing the linens for the whole family – *Mamm, Daed,* Nicole, Mark, and their four younger siblings – was a mammoth task, but at this time of year, Nicole had to do it whenever the weather played along.

She hoped it would hold today. Stepping back, a little breathless, she squinted up at the sky. Still clear.

"Your *mudder* said I'd find you here."

Nicole turned, surprised to see Hamish walking across the backyard toward her, his boots crunching on hard-packed snow. She picked up the basket, tucking it under her arm, and offered him a smile.

"I didn't know I'd be seeing you today," she said.

"I've been planning this for a while." There was something twitchy in his smile. "Is there somewhere we can talk alone, out of the wind?"

She stared at him for a few moments, remembering the way he'd stared at Viviana. Was he going to tell her that he didn't want to court her anymore? Her stomach swooped at the thought, but she smiled past it.

"Everyone's in the *haus*, except Mark, who's taken the stable for the Christmas program to the school," said Nicole. "So we could talk in the barn, if you don't mind. Mark asked me to take the horses' blankets off anyway."

Hamish shrugged. "That's all right. I'll help you."

She put the laundry basket through the back door, and they walked to the barn together. Something seemed to be hanging between them, an invisible curtain in the cold air. Nicole swallowed a few times in a bid to loosen the clenched nervousness in her stomach, but it didn't work.

When they stepped into the barn, she was almost desperate to stall him. "*Mamm* and my *shvestahs* are going to get started on the Christmas baking this week," she said conversationally, opening a stall door and going inside. The buggy horse nudged her shoulder affectionately as she began to undo the buckles of his thick stable rug.

"That's nice. Are you going to help?" Hamish asked. He took off his hat and wiped at his brow despite the biting cold.

"Of course. We're going to make some of those iced sugar cookies you like. Shepherds and sheep, stars and stables, camels and wise men." Nicole knew she was blathering and stopped.

"Nicole." Hamish took this as his cue. With a deep breath, he leaned on the stall door. "I need to talk to you about something important."

She stripped off the blanket and held it in her arms, feeling the horse's warmth still in the fabric. Despite the fine hairs covering the blanket, she hugged it a little closer, as if for comfort.

"*Jah?*" she managed breathlessly.

Hamish squared his shoulders, looking her firmly in the eye. "I think it's time we talked about marriage."

The horse blanket fell to the ground with a slap. Nicole bent to pick it up quickly, her hands shaking as she pulled it into her arms, then stared up at Hamish again. The word *marriage* seemed to hang in the air above his head, giant and inescapable.

"M-marriage?" she breathed.

"*Jah*." Hamish smiled, tipping up his chin. "I think you're a fine woman, Nicole. You'll be a *gut* wife and mother. I spoke to your *vadder*, and he's in favor. So I wanted to know what you thought about getting published now and marrying next fall, when the harvest is in."

Nicole opened and shut her mouth a few times, seeking words. In many ways, her entire life had been preparation for this moment. This was supposed to be the pinnacle of her youth; courting, engagement, and finally, marriage. The beginning of her true Amish womanhood. She'd been waiting for this for months, dreamed of this moment over and over again, and now she was here, and it didn't feel like a pinnacle. It felt... disorienting. She was flat-footed, unbalanced, as though caught unaware on black ice.

She took a deep breath, trying to find the words, but Hamish spoke before she could. "I've already arranged with my *vadder* that I will build a *haus* on the other side of the farm. It would be small at first, but once we have *kinner*, I can always extend it."

Children. Nicole's belly swooped, and she felt a sudden and desperate knowledge that she didn't want children with Hamish. And if not children, then how could there be marriage? Panic and pain clashed in her heart.

"I... I..." Nicole cleared her throat, hanging the blanket over the stall door. "I don't know what to say."

Hamish frowned. "Why? You're already nineteen. I thought you wanted to get married quickly."

"I suppose I do," said Nicole. She swallowed. "It's just – a bit of a surprise, that's all."

"Why would it be?" Hamish demanded. "Why else do you think I've been courting you?"

She stared at him. *It's a surprise because of the way you looked at Viviana at the library the other day.* But she couldn't say it.

"I know. I'm not – I'm not saying *nee*." Nicole swallowed. "Perhaps I just need a little time to think about it. To get used to the idea."

Hamish stepped back, his hands falling to his sides. "So you want to wait?"

"I... don't know."

"You have to give me an answer." Hamish folded his arms. "You can't keep me on a line forever."

"I know." Nicole meant for the words to come out gently, but they didn't. She took a deep breath, said them again, this time with more sweetness. "I know. I won't make you wait long. I just need to get used to the idea, like I said."

He gave her a long, suspicious look, then shook his head. "I don't understand."

"I... don't understand either." Nicole mustered a smile. "Please. I just need some time to think. Maybe... give me until Christmas Day. I'll tell you then, after church."

Hamish sighed, his shoulders sagging. "All right. If that's what you want."

He turned on his heel and strode away, and Nicole watched him go, her heart lodged firmly in her boots.

Chapter Eight

Sitting in the back of the buggy, Nicole stole another glance at the note in her hand. It was the same as all the others had been: on cheap paper, scribbled carelessly with no real form.

Hey Nicky. Are you getting these? It's been really fun writing them. Hope you're enjoying the snowshoes and keeping warm. How's your friend Hamish? I'm pretty bored now that I'm off work this week. Let me know if it would be okay for me to come and see you. Bye.

"We're here," said *Daed* suddenly from the front of the buggy. "I'll pick you up at four, Nicole."

"*Danke, Daedi.*" Nicole quickly folded up the note and stuffed it between the pages of one of the books she was returning, along with the other notes. There had been four more, and each one added to the tightness in her chest.

Daed put out a hand and touched her arm as she was about to disembark, his eyes searching hers. "Are you all right, *liebchen*? You've seemed a little distant since yesterday, when Hamish came to see you."

Mamm shot him a sharp look, and Nicole mustered a smile. She didn't want to talk about this with her father. He had, after all, given Hamish his blessing to ask her about marriage. That must mean that he liked him.

"I'm fine, *danke*," she said quietly. "I'll see you at four."

He let go of her arm. "See you."

Walking quickly, Nicole hurried into the library. She took the letters out of her book and kept them tucked under her arm as she quickly returned the books, then went straight to the table where she always sat with Viviana. To her profound relief, Viviana was alone. She was sitting back in her chair, paging through a cookbook and looking much more relaxed than before, although her earphones were still in.

"Hello, Viviana," said Nicole, sliding into the chair opposite her.

Viviana pulled out an earphone. "Oh, hey. No Hamish today?" Her voice rang with disappointment.

Nicole stared at her for a few moments, dismay spreading through her chest. But... well, did Viviana know that she and Hamish were courting? She hadn't told her anything. Surely, if she told Viviana, she would stop acting so strange over him.

"*Nee*," she managed, clearing her throat and taking the letters out from under her arm. They were a more pressing problem.

"Aw, okay." Viviana sat back. "Hey, check out these Christmas recipes. Some of them are supposed to be Amish."

Nicole leaned over and glanced at the book. "*Jah*, this looks like the chocolate pie we often make for Christmas."

"No fruit cake?" asked Viviana, surprised.

"Fruit cake, too." Nicole smiled, relieved that Viviana seemed back to her usual self. "We cook quite a feast. In fact, we're starting the baking next week."

"Sounds like a ton of work." Viviana laughed. "Mom just goes to the market and buys things ready-made."

"*Jah*, I suppose it is a lot of work, but it's always a fun time for us." Nicole grinned. "We laugh and joke and sing and it's precious family time with my *mamm* and sisters."

"Sounds special." Viviana sighed, tucking some of her hair behind her ear. "Mom and Dad are always saying we should spend more time together as a family, but we just end up sitting around awkwardly or fighting over board games. Or on our phones." She shrugged. "I guess you're lucky in that way. You get to see the people you love because everyone lives close by."

"I guess." Nicole bit her lip, looking down at the letters. "Viviana, I need to ask you about… well… Chad."

THE CHRISTMAS SNOWSHOES

"Chad?" Viviana raised her eyebrows. "Why?"

"Well, I've been getting these... notes," said Nicole reluctantly. She pushed them toward her. "From him."

"I wondered why he wanted to know your home address." Viviana laughed, glancing over the notes. "Look at you, Nicky. Seems like you've got a not-so-secret admirer."

"Don't laugh," said Nicole, dismayed. "You don't understand. I'm Amish. It's not allowed."

Viviana gave her a long look. "Nicky, I'm sorry if my brother's made you uncomfortable, but I promise he never means any harm."

"I didn't think he did." Nicole hung her head, her cheeks burning with embarrassment. She had hoped this conversation would go very differently. Why did this have to be so complicated? She thought of the ride home in his truck that day, and her belly flipped as she remembered how easily she had laughed. If only things were as simple for her as they were for Viviana...

"Well, if you need to tell him to cut it out, go for it." Viviana nodded toward the doors and got up. "I'm heading to the restroom."

"What?" Nicole turned, disoriented, as Viviana hurried off. The library doors had swung open, letting in a gust of cold air, and Chad was walking into the library.

Nicole's heart plunged through her boots. The last thing she had wanted today was a face-to-face confrontation with Chad, especially if Viviana wasn't here. She didn't feel threatened by him, but she had a feeling this was going to be extremely awkward.

She tried to grab all the letters before he reached the table, but one of them escaped as he flopped into the chair beside hers, skidding across the table toward him. He reached out and stopped it, then looked up at her with a wide grin.

"So you *have* been getting them," he said triumphantly.

"I have," Nicole squeaked. "Chad, I – "

"It's okay. I didn't really expect you to write back. I just…" His cheeks reddened bashfully, and he dropped his eyes. "I just wanted you to know I was thinking of you."

Nicole tried not to look at the way his dusky pink lips curved downward over the shadow of his dark blond stubble. She swallowed, calming herself. There was a very straightforward way out of this, she reminded herself.

"They were sweet of you," she said, slowly, "but there's a reason I didn't write back."

He looked up at her, his eyes fearful. "I don't want to drag you away from your farm life, or whatever," he said quickly. "Just maybe get to know you a little better, that's all."

"That's not possible," said Nicole as gently as she could.

"Why? Because you're Amish?" Chad looked hurt. "Are there rules against being friends with someone non-Amish?"

"Not friends, no," said Nicole hesitantly. "It's not about the *Ordnung*... our rules for living. It's about – well – someone else in my life."

Chad glanced swiftly at her hands. "I didn't realize you guys married so young."

"I'm not married." Nicole let her hands slide into her lap, knowing it would be useless to explain to Chad that the Amish didn't wear rings. "But I am... engaged." She flinched over the word. "Practically engaged," she amended.

"Practically engaged?" Chad's cocky grin returned, and he sank back into his chair. "Well, that's the same as dating, right? You're fair game."

"What? *Nee.*" Confusion bubbled in Nicole's heart, and she stared at him. "How can that be true? *Nee*, Chad, I'm – I'm not *fair game*, I'm – "

"Relax, Nicky." Chad held up both hands. "I'm just saying that if you're only dating, things could change. And I can wait."

Nicole stared at him, struggling for words. She tried to imagine a young Amish man even suggesting courtship to a girl who already had someone courting her. It was absolutely unthinkable. It felt like Chad thought he could steal her away like an object.

She was reminded, sharply, how different the *Englisch* world was from the Amish one. And she knew with sudden, blinding certainty in which world she actually belonged.

"It can't work," she said firmly. "You're *Englisch*. It's forbidden."

Disappointment covered Chad's face. He opened his mouth to argue, but at that moment Viviana popped out of one of the aisles, clutching a huge cookbook.

"Chad," she squealed. "Remember those *crazy* good mince pies that Auntie Petunia always made for us before she died? This recipe looks just like them."

Grateful for the interruption, Nicole let out a breath, crumpling up the letters and shoving them into the wastepaper basket by her side when Chad wasn't looking. She realized, then, with sharp agony, that she had forgotten to give back the snowshoes.

∼

Nicole squinted down at the cookie in front of her, concentrating, her hands steady on the piping bag. Carefully, she traced a white outline around the little shape of the sweet sugar cookie: an angel, his wings spreading on either side, his robe billowing around him.

"Aw, look at them," cried her younger sister, Sarah, leaning over her shoulder. "They're so beautiful."

"And they look delicious," added her younger brother, Charlie. He grabbed at one, and Nicole slapped his hand away, laughing. "Stop that," she said. "They're definitely delicious, and you know it. You stole enough cookie dough to know that."

Charlie giggled in a manner that suggested that more cookies would go missing soon anyway. Nicole laughed and sighed in the same breath.

Mamm and her other sister, Gertie, were hard at work icing the camels beside her. Gertie sang softly and steadily in her high, piping voice. "Angels we have heard on high/sweetly singing o'er the plains/and the mountains in reply/echoing their joyous strains."

Nicole lifted her voice to join in with the chorus, their voices blending perfectly and sailing through the air over the rows of brightly iced cookies that lay over the kitchen table. Nicole's voice was warm and rounded, easily complementing Gertie's pure tones. *Gloria in excelsis Deo.*

Nicole's heart felt filled with warmth as the song came to an end and she slapped Charlie's wayward hand away from another cookie. She set the angel aside, grabbed another and started icing its outline, thinking about what that moment must have been like. A moment when the entire night lit up with glory, and the very sky trembled with the strength of the angels' joyous song. She thought, not for the first time, that she would have given anything to be one of those shepherds;

tending sheep on a dark night one moment, irresistibly thrust into something splendid and magical the next.

"Christmas is amazing," said Sarah, grinning widely, her joy written loudly on her face. "I love it so much."

"Well, love it while you get on with frosting the little stables, dear," said *Mamm*, "or we'll never finish these."

"I don't want to finish them," said Gertie. "I love icing cookies together. It might be my favorite part of Christmas."

"Mine, too," said Nicole. "I love baking with you all."

"That's sweet of you, my *dochtahs*." *Mamm* smiled, her eyes tired, but her cheeks rosy. "It's an honor to be here with you, too."

Nicole felt a sudden sting of tears behind her eyes. She bent over the angel, wondering what her next Christmas would look like. She tried to picture herself sitting in a cozy little kitchen of her own, the fire crackling, icing sugar cookies, Hamish enjoying a cup of coffee nearby. Instead of feeling a rush of excitement, the only thing in her heart was a rising dread.

She shook her head faintly, carrying on with her frosting. Nonsense. Of course, she was looking forward to her first Christmas as a married woman, assuming she said yes to Hamish... but she was going to say yes to him? Of course, she was. This was what she was supposed to do, wasn't it? So why did it make her heart sting to think of it?

Her thoughts wandered back to the day Stephen had driven her home, to the way he had laughed at himself. She pulled her thoughts back. Why was she thinking about Stephen?

She shook her head, sliding the completed angel sugar cookie to one side. She could only wish that this Christmas could be as clear as the skies had been on the night the angels sang. Silently, she prayed God would clear away the blizzard in her heart.

~

"Phew." *Daed* let out an audible breath of relief as he brought the buggy to a halt outside the schoolyard, its wheels squawking on the slippery ground. "I'm glad we made it. We almost had to walk."

Nicole stepped out of the buggy very carefully, her boots gripping the icy surface. She decided not to mention that snowshoes would have made this easier. Then again, maybe they wouldn't. There was little snow on the ground, but it was so cold that everything seemed to have frozen solid. Icicles hung from the schoolyard fence and from the eaves of the little schoolhouse itself; her boots slipped and crunched on the ground, and as the community headed into the schoolhouse, she could see grandmothers and grandfathers clinging to the sturdy arms of young men to keep from falling.

Stephen had a grandparent on each arm. Joan and her husband, David, were both hanging onto him for dear life as he approached the schoolhouse, but his strong frame seemed unaffected by their weight. He was moving slowly, one little step at a time, but there was no sign of frustration in his face. Instead, Nicole heard a wisp of laughter drift back to her from them.

"Nicole," said *Mamm* smoothly, "why don't you go and help Stephen with his *groossmammi*? He must be struggling with them both."

She glanced over at *Mamm*, surprised. "I think he's all right. I'd like to sit with you." She hadn't been sorry to hear that Hamish had a cold and wasn't coming to the program, even though that thought filled her with guilt.

Mamm gave a secretive little smile. "I think Stephen needs your help more than we do right now."

Nicole gave her father a bewildered look, but he didn't protest, so she scrambled across the slippery schoolyard to Stephen. He was finally starting to look a little strained now as Joan's shoes slipped on the ice and she clutched at him tightly with a little squeal of dismay; at the same moment, David lost his walking stick, and seized Stephen's coat with both hands.

"Here, David." Nicole quickly picked up the stick and handed it to the old man.

"*Ach, danke.*" David gasped in relief, finding his balance again.

"Hello, Nicole." Stephen's voice was slightly strained, but his smile was genuine. "*Danke* for the help. These two old bats are getting to be a bit of a handful."

"*Ach*," cried Joan, but they all three laughed, and the love between them was a palpable thing in the cold air.

"Can I offer an arm, Joan?" Nicole asked, holding her arm out to the old lady.

"*Danke, liebchen.*" Joan gripped her arm tightly and gave her a sparkling smile. "Let's go on inside, shall we?"

"*Jah*, let's get you out of the cold," said Stephen.

Even without the fire crackling in a small wood stove at the corner of the schoolhouse, the little building would have been very warm, packed as it was with the benches and containing almost everyone from the community. Nicole and Stephen steered Joan and David into some empty seats near the front row; Stephen had two younger cousins in the program, and they were eager to see them. They sat down on either side of his grandparents, Joan and David holding hands.

A little out of breath, Nicole took the opportunity to gaze around the schoolhouse, and gasped with joy. It was beautifully decorated. Plain garland hung all around the walls, along with paper chains the children had made from brightly colored construction paper. The blackboard had been taken down for the occasion and replaced by a backdrop painted with the Star of Bethlehem and a quiet, moonlit landscape. In pride of place, front and center, stood the manger that Mark and Stephen had built. It had been lined with straw.

"I love your manger," Nicole whispered to Stephen over his grandparents' bent heads.

He grinned at her. "All our hard work is paying off. Your *brudder* did most of it."

"Well, he was certainly glad of your help." Nicole smiled. "I think this is going to be the best Christmas program yet."

In many ways, it was. The little boy playing Gabriel didn't make any allusion to what flavor Mary might be (David elbowed Stephen gently in the ribs and grinned mischievously at this point, making Stephen roll his eyes with mock despair); the girls sang beautifully, especially Sarah. The little kids playing the shepherds looked suitably terrified, and in the end, the Nativity scene – complete with someone's pet lamb, although the Hochstetlers had left their donkey at home this year – was a picture.

It struck Nicole, watching the eighth-grader who played Mary cradling her little brother who was playing Baby Jesus, that the real Virgin Mary had been no older than this child when she had given birth to the Savior of the World. She wondered if the night had been as cold as this one. She wondered if the stable had been as warm as this schoolhouse, and if the manger had been lined with straw as clean as this. A shiver ran down her spine as the children sang, "Silent Night" together, their unaccompanied voices rising up till the rafters of the schoolhouse itself seemed to tremble.

The song ended on a last quivering note expertly delivered by Sarah, and applause broke out among the community. Stephen enthusiastically joined in. The children ran off to their parents, Mark bundled away the manger with obvious pride on his face, and the schoolhouse was filled with chatter.

"Your *shvestah*'s voice is amazing," said Stephen as they made their way through the crowd and out into the frigid night. People everywhere were laughing, talking, congratulating small children in costume on their performances.

"*Danke*. She's very *gut*." Nicole laughed. "She was so nervous, but I think she did a *wunderlich* job."

"The Lantz *maidels* have always had *gut* voices," said Joan approvingly. "I remember when your *groossmammi* – your *daed's mamm* – was young, and we went to sings together. She always had flocks of young boys around her because of her voice."

"*Groossmammi*," laughed Stephen. "Wait here – I'll get the horse." He hurried to fetch the horse from where it waited, tied to a hitching post with a nosebag of oats to keep it busy.

"*Ach*, I used to be jealous of her." Joan grinned, looking back at Nicole, her eyes bright and wise in the starlight. "I believed that I would never find the right husband because she was taking all the attention. But you know what?"

"What?" asked Nicole.

"It didn't matter if I couldn't sing." Joan looked fondly at David. "When the time was right, I found the perfect man."

David smiled at her, squeezing her hand, and even though their faces were both deeply wrinkled and their voices creaky with age, in that moment they both looked as young and radiant as they had been on their wedding day.

Chapter Nine

❦

It was December 22nd, the day before the youth dinner, and Nicole sat at the kitchen table with her hands working quickly. The Scrabble box lay beside her, and she was counting out the ivory tiles, lining them up in neat rows of the same letter, her fingers flying. A to-do list lay on the table in front of her. Suddenly, it seemed as though she'd never have enough time for everything.

"Busy, I see," said Gertie, coming into the kitchen. "I thought you were going to the library today."

"*Nee.*" Nicole felt a pang of regret and sorrow. "I think I need a little time away from... the library." She thought of the two notes Chad had written to her since last week. She'd burned them both.

"*Ach*, that's a pity. You love the library." Gertie peered into the oven. "You've been at home all on your own for nearly a week now. Maybe Hamish should come and take you for a drive – or you'll forget that it's Christmas at all."

Nicole didn't say she didn't feel much like Christmas this year. She added an E to a long row of letters and shrugged. "I think Hamish still has a cold."

"*Nee*, he doesn't. He was at church on Sunday, remember?" Gertie paused midway through taking a mince pie out of the oven. She cocked her head slightly to one side, steam rising around her face from the pie. "What's going on with you two, anyway?"

Nicole looked up at Gertie, feeling her cheeks warm. "Wh- what do you mean?"

Gertie set the mince pie down on the table and closed the oven. "Come now, Nicole. I'm not blind, you know," she said affectionately. "You can talk to me."

Nicole sighed, looking down at the tiles. She moved an N into place. "Hamish talked to me about marriage."

"Marriage." Gertie raised her eyebrows. "Did you say *jah*?"

Nicole sighed. "I said I needed time to think."

"*Gut*," said Gertie. "Because I think you should think very hard."

"Why would you say that?" asked Nicole.

"Because I think you need to be very sure that you truly love someone before you agree to marry them," said Gertie succinctly. Before Nicole could say anything more, she strode out of the room.

Nicole sighed, staring down at the row of Ls. *Truly love someone*. Her heart sank. Did she truly love Hamish? Would she know what true love was, even if she felt it? Hamish was good enough. Perhaps good enough would do.

There was a knock at the door, startling her out of her reverie, and she was surprised to see a tall figure step inside. "Morning, Nicole."

"Oh... hello, Stephen." Nicole's heart slowed. For a second, she'd been worried it was Hamish. "How are you?"

"I'm all right." Stephen smiled. "Is Mark around?"

"*Nee*, he's gone into town with *Daed*." Nicole grimaced. "Sorry."

"It's all right. I'll see him later – he said he'd help me get the schoolhouse ready for the youth dinner." Stephen pulled off his hat and ran a hand through his hair. "I just wanted to ask him to bring a few things tomorrow."

"You can make a list, and I'll tell him."

"*Danke*." Stephen pulled a list from his pocket, glancing at the Scrabble tiles. "What are you doing?"

"Making sure we have all the pieces for all the board games." Nicole smiled. "I wouldn't want any of tomorrow's games to be ruined."

"*Gut* thinking." Stephen laughed, then sneezed loudly.

"*Ach, nee*," said Nicole. "Don't tell me you've got it, too."

"Got what?" Stephen rubbed his nose.

"That flu that's been doing the rounds. Hamish had it lightly. Sarah's still quite sick with it, and I had a runny nose for a few days." Nicole finished counting the tiles and swept them all into the bag.

Stephen looked away at the mention of Hamish. "*Jah*, I also just had a cough for a day or two. But my poor grandparents are both pretty sick."

"*Ach, nee*. Sorry to hear that. Are they going to be all right?"

"I'm sure they will be." Stephen smiled. "They just need lots of nursing. I've put them both to bed, and I'm keeping them warm." His smile slipped. "I just don't think I'm going to make it to the dinner."

"But you put so much work into it," Nicole exclaimed. "You can't miss out on it now."

"*Ach*, well. I just want to make sure my grandparents are all right." Stephen shrugged, smiling crookedly.

"I'm so sorry." Nicole sighed. "I'm disappointed for you. You put so much effort into this."

"*Ach*, you know, the work was its own reward." Stephen's eyes held her for a second before looking away.

"Will your grandparents be all right?" Nicole asked. "Do you need anything for them? Medicine, maybe?"

"*Nee, danke*, we'll be fine. As soon as I've told Mark what he needs to do to take care of my part of tomorrow's arrangements, I'll drive to town and get them some oatmeal and the herbal tea they like."

Nicole got up, opening a cabinet. "I've got oatmeal for you. What kind of tea do they want? Chamomile?"

"Peppermint," said Stephen, "but don't worry."

"*Ach*, I'm sorry. We only have chamomile." Nicole turned back to him. "I can give you the oatmeal, though. We have plenty."

"*Nee, danke*. It's all right." Stephen smiled. "I need to go to town anyway, and it's not far from the schoolhouse. I'll get them some."

"You'll tell me if I can do anything to help, right?" said Nicole.

He smiled again, and she felt something flutter – something inexplicable deep in the pit of her chest. Something she had never felt before. It was unsettling and glorious, and it made her palms sweat.

"I will. But I'm sure we'll be fine. *Danke* so much for your concern." Stephen laid a hand on the front door, ready to leave.

"Stephen?" said Nicole, quickly.

He looked back at her, his smile still on his face.

"You'll be safe, won't you?" she said. "The dinner won't really be the same without you."

He grinned back. "Don't worry. I'll be just fine."

~

"Listen to that wind," *Mamm* said, shaking her head as she sat in her rocking chair just an hour later. Her knitting needles clicked rhythmically, even though she was looking out of the window. "It looks like that storm they've been forecasting has come early."

Nicole was packing the games into a bag to send to the schoolhouse with Mark. She looked worriedly out of the living room window. Outside, the landscape lay flat and gray underneath a sky that seemed so low it almost touched the ground. The trees bucked and tossed madly in the wind; a loose piece of roofing clanged disconsolately on the barn, and the howl of the wind was throaty and fierce around the eaves of the house.

"I hope *Daed* and Mark get home from town soon," said *Mamm*. "Soon there won't be any traveling in this."

"*Ach, nee*," said Nicole softly.

Mamm raised an eyebrow. "Were you planning on going somewhere this evening?"

"*Nee*, not really. I know Mark wanted to go to the schoolhouse to meet with Stephen, though." Nicole sighed. "And poor Stephen's grandparents have the flu. He was here earlier with a message for Mark, and he said he was going to town this afternoon to get them some oatmeal and herbal tea."

"He certainly won't be able to do it now," said *Mamm* regretfully. "Did you give him some oatmeal?"

"I tried, but he said he'd go to town for it." Nicole set the games bag down on the coffee table and stared out at the wild, gray afternoon. Stephen's home was just a few miles away across those fields. She should go over there. She didn't know why she was suddenly so sure of this.

Before she could speak, though, the front door banged open, and Mark came stumbling into the living room. He tossed his snow-covered coat over a chair and hurried in front of the fire, plucking off his mittens. When he tucked his mittens under his arm, Nicole heard them crackle with ice. He held out his hands to the fire and groaned, shivering.

"It's terrible out there. Terrible," he said. "The storm's pretty much on top of us. It's so cold out there."

"Are the animals safe in the barn?" asked *Mamm*, lowering her knitting needles.

"*Jah*, they're all fine. We put a canvas over the hay, too. Everything here is fine." Mark sighed regretfully, staring out of the window. "I just don't know if I'm going to make it to the schoolhouse."

Similarly shivering and covered in snow, *Daed* came into the living room as Mark was speaking, and he immediately shook his head.

"There's no way you're going to the schoolhouse today," he said sharply. "The roads will be completely impassable, and besides, how would you get back? This is only going to intensify."

Mark sighed. "I know you're right, *Daed*. I just have to take some things there for tomorrow."

Daed rested a hand on Mark's shoulder and cast a sympathetic glance at Nicole. "I know you two have been looking forward to this, but I doubt the dinner will be happening at all tomorrow. It's just foolishness for anyone to be out in weather like this. It's not worth the risk."

Nicole felt an unexpected pang of sharp disappointment. She looked at the bag of games on the coffee table. She and Stephen would have been such good Pictionary partners...

She shook her head faintly. No, she and *Hamish* would have been good Pictionary partners. She was going to marry him, after all. Wasn't she?

"It's disappointing," Mark was saying, "but there's not much we can do about it." He gave Nicole an encouraging smile. "We can play games here at home."

"That's a *gut* idea." *Mamm* resumed her knitting. "Don't unpack the games yet, Nicole."

"*Jah, Mamm*." Nicole hesitated. "Do you think I could take some oatmeal over to Stephen's *haus*?"

"Not now, with the storm coming down so hard," said *Daed* firmly. "Maybe later, if it's looking better. But I doubt we'll be able to get the buggy out for days. Get ready to be snowed in."

Nicole turned away as Mark and *Daed* headed upstairs to change. She walked up to the window and rested her hands on the sill, staring. The snow was coming down thickly now, swirling and gusting in the wind.

And she wished she knew why she felt as though her heart was caught up in that wind, blowing across the snowy fields to Stephen's house.

Chapter Ten

The wild howl of the wind had abated. Nicole lay in bed, curled on her side, gazing out of her window. There was a gas lamp over her window, and it shone out onto the snowy fields. Fat, white flakes were drifting down steadily, their slight patter quiet on the roof of the house, falling straight down in a white curtain. She could see only a few yards before the snow and darkness swallowed her vision.

Pulling her quilt up over her shoulders, Nicole closed her eyes and tried again to stop thinking about David and Joan and Stephen. She remembered the dancing laughter in the old lady's eyes, and the wisdom in David's stern expression. And she remembered the way Stephen laughed with them like they were his best friends instead of just old people he'd been burdened with. She didn't think she'd ever seen someone love like that before.

Now he would be all alone in that cold house, trying to nurse his grandparents back to health without even the oatmeal and herbal tea that they liked.

Nicole's eyes snapped open again. She stared at the snow. It was coming down steadily, but not that hard anymore. *Daed* was probably right when he said that it would snow for more than a day, but at least with the wind gone, the visibility was better. It was late, but perhaps Nicole could still hitch up the buggy and drive that way...

She sat up in bed, going over to the window, and peered down at the yard. Her heart sank. The lower two feet of the barn doors were already submerged in snow. Just shoveling a path to the barn and getting the buggy out would take ages. Actually, driving it was unthinkable.

There was no way to move along the road, not with the soft, fluffy snow so deep.

She straightened suddenly. Deep snow. *The snowshoes feel funny on your feet, but once you get the hang of walking in them, it's pretty cool to walk around on deep snow that you'd normally fall into.* Viviana's words rang around her mind.

She could make it to Stephen's house on her snowshoes.

Her mind was made up, with a sudden clarity she'd never felt before. She pulled on her thickest dress and several pairs of socks, then her best boots and coat, mittens and scarf, and she pulled her outer *kapp* over her ears. Tiptoeing out into the hallway, she glanced at her parents' room. The crack under their doorway was dark. They were asleep.

They'd be annoyed, Nicole guessed, but she had a feeling *Mamm* would understand.

Hurrying down the stairs, Nicole grabbed a pen and paper from the living room and scrawled a note. *Going to the Bylers on snowshoes. Back when it's daylight. Love, Nicole.*

Then she squared her shoulders and stepped out into the snow.

∽

It was only with the help of a shovel and a lot of determination that Nicole fought her way across the yard to the overhang where the buggy stood. Snow had blown in underneath the tin roof, lying several inches deep around the buggy wheels, but despite the bitter cold and the constant trickle of snow, Nicole was breathless and sweating by the time she reached it. She leaned the shovel against the wall and opened the back of the buggy, and they were still lying there. The snowshoes and the two poles.

She sat on the backseat, legs hanging out of the buggy, and pulled on the snowshoes one by one. They felt huge and clumsy on her feet as before, but when she gripped the poles and stood up, her coordination seemed to come back to her. She closed the buggy door and took a few shuffling steps forward, swinging her feet wide to avoid stepping on the snowshoes. The poles sank into the snow, far deeper than it had been in Viviana's backyard that day, but when she stepped out with the snowshoes, she found herself sinking just an inch or two despite the fact the snow was nearly two feet deep.

Nicole grinned, her laughter coming out on clouds of steam. She wiped some snow off her face and turned toward the west. The quickest way to get to Stephen's house would be not to follow the road, but to walk along the leeward side of the stone wall. The snow was fractionally lower here, and while she'd have to clamber over a post-and-rail fence or two, she could go straight across the fields to his house.

She had brought along a flashlight. She switched it on, and the blue-white beam cut through the snow to show a few yards ahead of her. A few yards was enough for her. She'd make this journey a few steps at a time. She adjusted the strap of the satchel over her shoulder, containing the bag of oatmeal and the box of chamomile tea—even though it wasn't peppermint, gritted her teeth, and set off.

The snow piled thickly onto her eyelashes. She kept having to shake her head or brush a mittened hand over her eyes to get rid of them. Cold nipped painfully at her nose for the first few minutes, until it turned completely numb. The snow crunched under her feet, and the sky was absolutely black, but the snowshoes worked, and she kept moving at a steady pace, her heart thudding in her chest.

When she reached the fence of the first field, Nicole's legs and hips were already aching persistently from the way she had to walk with the snowshoes on. At least the exercise was warming her, but she could feel her face going numb, and her fingers stung despite her mittens. She stopped then to look back, and saw absolutely nothing in any direction except for snow, wall, and fence. A low hill had swallowed up even the lights of her parents' house. She felt suddenly and completely alone.

Terror flooded through her, and she clutched at the strap of her satchel, her heart thudding painfully in her chest.

You're not alone, dochtah.

The voice came from somewhere deep within, somewhere far beyond Christmas. Nicole took a deep breath and turned her face back toward the fence, then gripped the post in both hands, closing her eyes. *Gott, I need You,* she whispered in her soul.

She gripped the fence, pulled herself over it, and went on, and there was new purpose in her steps now. The snow was still coming down, and the night was still very black, and the cold was still bitter, but as she moved, it felt as though each step lent her strength. She dug the poles into the ground with each step, remembering Viviana's sweet laughter as she had stumbled around the backyard on that sunny afternoon. A smile played on her lips. Viviana had always been good to her, no matter what Chad had in mind.

Her elbow brushed the stone wall by her side. It had been skillfully put together decades, perhaps centuries ago by skilled Amish hands, hands that had worked in the same way that her father and brothers worked to this very day, fueled by women who had cooked the same recipes she did.

Perhaps, she thought, her life didn't have to be about one or the other. Perhaps it was like Stephen had said: her life could just be about God, and that would be enough.

It felt as though the snow, the cold, the hardship, the struggle were wiping away all of the things that had been worrying her so much. Chad. Hamish. What her parents thought. She felt as though there was nothing in the world except for the next step, the light upon her path, and the Spirit inside her. And it was then that she felt her rising eagerness to reach Stephen's house. Her excitement to get there, to look into his eyes, to help him.

∾

At last, incredibly, she saw the golden pool of a gas lamp – the lamp above Stephen's door. Nicole clambered over the last fence, breathing heavily, with a rising sense of relief. Her legs felt as though they would scarcely bear her another step.

She stumbled up onto the front porch. Late though it was, the gas lights in the kitchen were on, and she could see a figure moving around, silhouetted against the drawn curtains. Raising her mittened hand, she pounded hard on the door, breathless and gripped with a sudden fear that no one would open the door, and she would never get out of this snow.

The figure disappeared, and the door opened almost instantly. Nicole looked up into a pair of startled brown eyes.

"Nicole," Stephen gasped. He stared at her for just one second, then grasped her arm gently and pulled her into the warmth of the kitchen, closing the door behind her. "You must be half frozen."

She realized she was, and that the warmth of the room felt like it was scorching her skin. Or maybe that was just the fact she was standing suddenly very close to Stephen in the doorway, looking up into his eyes. He smelled like cinnamon and pine trees for some reason. Her heart turned a slow somersault in her chest.

Their closeness lasted just a moment. Then Stephen was bustling into the kitchen, tossing more wood onto the fire, lighting the gas hob underneath the kettle. "What are you doing here?" he cried, pulling out a chair for her.

Nicole stumbled over to it and sank down gratefully, reaching down with shaking hands to take off her snowshoes. Even when she'd pulled off her mittens, her hands felt slow and stupid with cold, and she couldn't undo the buckles. Stephen was kneeling beside her in a moment, unbuckling the snowshoes and pulling them off. His hands were quick and gentle.

"I – I brought you s-s-some oatmeal," she stammered out past chattering teeth. She unhooked the satchel's strap from her shoulder, wincing at how cold it was. The cloth crackled with ice.

"Oatmeal?" Stephen took it, staring up at her. "You came all this way for oatmeal?"

Nicole shrugged. "You said your g-g-g-grandparents liked it."

"*Ach*, Nicole." Stephen's eyes softened as he set the satchel down on the table. "I can't tell you how much this means to me. I… I haven't been able to get them to eat all day. Truth be told, I was getting desperate." His eyes shone. "*Danke* so much for coming."

Nicole's heart leapt within her. She would have stared into his eyes for much too long, but he turned away then and set her snowshoes by the front door, letting out a little laugh. "I see your snowshoes turned out to be useful after all."

"They did." Nicole grinned. "I must remember to thank Viviana and tell her the whole story when I see her at the library next week." She realized she was looking forward to it.

The kettle was boiling. Nicole got up, feeling better already, and flipped open the satchel. "I'm sorry I didn't have peppermint tea, but I brought the chamomile in case they'd want it."

"Maybe they will. *Danke*," said Stephen again, taking the box from her. "I haven't been able to get anything into them other than some hot milk." His face was pinched with worry, and Nicole noticed how very pale he was.

She moved around the table to join him by the stove and rested a hand on his arm. The movement felt easy, natural. "I'm here to help you now," she said.

Their eyes met, and his smile seemed to light up corners of her soul she hadn't even known she had.

∼

"Just another sip or two, Joan," Nicole encouraged softly. She steadied the teacup in Joan's shaky hands. "I'm sure you'll be able to sleep once you've finished your tea."

Joan's eyes were very red, and her breathing rattled as she tipped up the cup and drained the last of the tea. "Ahh," she breathed, her voice hoarse and raspy, handing back the cup. "*Danke, dochtah*. That does feel a bit better."

Nicole touched Joan's forehead softly. "You're a little cooler now. I think the medicine is working."

"I'll be just fine, *liebchen*." Joan sank back onto her pillows, allowing Nicole to adjust the covers around her shoulders. She smiled up at her. "You came a very long way on snowshoes to help my grandson, didn't you?"

Nicole felt her cheeks redden. "Don't try to talk too much, Joan. Your throat must be very sore."

Joan let out a soft chuckle.

"I've been praying for this day for years," she said quietly, then closed her eyes before Nicole could ask her what she meant.

She thought perhaps she did know, though, when she closed the bedroom door quietly behind her and found Stephen was coming up the hallway toward her. When his eyes found hers, they were soft and very deep, and she felt her heart beat a little slower and more surely when she saw them.

"How are they?" he asked quietly. There was snow on his shoulders, and he carried an armful of wood for the bedroom fire.

"David's asleep, and I think your *groossmammi* is about to go to sleep, too. Their fevers have broken for now." Nicole smiled. "They seem much better than when I got here."

"*Danke* so much, Nicole. I don't know what I would have done without you." Stephen lowered the wood into the box by the bedroom door. "I'll come back and stoke the fire when I'm sure they're sleeping soundly."

"All right." Nicole took him gently by the elbow and steered him toward the kitchen. "And now I think it's time *you* had something to eat and drink. You look like you've been on your feet all day."

"I think I forgot dinner," Stephen confessed. "But I should be taking you home."

They headed downstairs into the kitchen, and Stephen twitched aside the curtains of the kitchen window. Outside, the wind had risen once more to a mournful howl, and the only thing visible outside was a wall of snowflakes blowing wildly through the air.

"I don't think we should be out in that," said Nicole nervously.

"Certainly not." Stephen let the curtains fall closed again. She was pouring him a cup of tea, and he sank into a chair slowly and stiffly.

"*Groossmammi* always keeps the spare room made up," he said. "You can stay there for the night."

"*Gut*. I know it's just down the hall from their room, so I can help you in the night." Nicole smiled at him. "I just hope my parents don't worry too much. I did leave them a note."

"They'll know you're safe with me," said Stephen softly, and when Nicole looked into his eyes, she knew it was absolutely true. Her parents *would* know, and they wouldn't worry, at least not too much.

She slid a mug of tea in front of him and sat down opposite him, sipping her own cup. The wind made its eerie music outside, but the kitchen crackled with warmth. Plain garland hung on the walls; the mantelpiece over the fire was filled with brightly colored Christmas cards. Nicole recognized the one that her younger sisters had made for the Bylers. *With Christmas blessings from the Lantz family.*

They sat drinking their tea together, and the silence wrapped around Nicole like a warm hug. It was a silence she didn't have to break. A silence in which her presence was enough. In which *she* was enough. A silence that seemed empty of all of her questions about who she was and where she belonged and what she was supposed to do about Hamish.

For in that silence, she knew all of her answers.

∽

Nicole set the steaming bowls of oatmeal down on the kitchen table just as David and Joan came down the stairs. When they walked into the kitchen, Stephen close behind them, she felt a smile leap spontaneously to her face.

"Merry Christmas," she cried.

"*Ach*. Of course." Joan met her eyes with a smile. "It's Christmas Eve."

Soft morning light filled the kitchen. The snow had stopped in the night, though it lay as deep as the windowsills around the cozy old farmhouse. David glanced at it as he sat down, wrapped in blankets and runny-nosed, but clearly interested in the oatmeal.

"Well, looks like you'll be staying with us until after Christmas," he said contentedly.

Nicole smiled. "Looks like it."

She sat down on Stephen's right hand. Their eyes met across the table, and Stephen gave her a happy, secret little smile. She felt something leap inside her. Something had forged that night while making tea, cold compresses for fevered foreheads, and honey milk for sore throats. Something had forged while carrying cough mixture and stoking the fire. Something deep and sure that rushed through her like a river.

"Let's take hands for grace," Stephen said.

She bowed her head, her fingers wrapped easily in his.

God had answered her prayer after all, for in that moment, her heart was as clear as the Christmas sky under the Star of Bethlehem.

The End

Continue Reading...

❦

Thank you for reading **The Christmas Snowshoes!** Are you wondering **what to read next?** Why not read **Runaway Christmas? Here's a peek for you:**

"We have to be out of this apartment by tomorrow because we can't pay the rent, and we have nowhere to go. And we don't have the money to find a new place, or to pay for anything else. I need to know what we're going to do." Marcy Sutton confronted her husband for the hundredth time, praying a miracle might suddenly present itself since Christmas was only a few weeks away.

But with his next words, an angrily hissed, "I don't know," Scott proved that looking to him for an answer was a mistake.

Marcy should have known better since he was the reason they were in this predicament in the first place. All their current troubles—from their imminent homelessness to the lurking threat posed by a loan shark's enforcers—could be traced back to her husband's actions.

Scott's face flushed red, as if he'd heard her thoughts, though they were not hard to guess, given this was far from the first confrontation between them about how his gambling was adversely affecting their family's increasingly precarious finances.

"What I do know, Marcy, is I'm not going to stand here while you blame me for everything that's gone wrong," he said without a smidgen of apparent guilt or regret.

Marcy wanted to shout back at him that this *was* all his fault, but she knew that would only escalate the situation further. Although it might feel good in the moment to vent her frustration and anger, it would solve nothing. Instead, it would only make the strain between them worse. She needed to stay calm if they were to have any chance of a rational conversation.

When she said nothing in response to his accusation, he turned on his heels and grabbed his coat from the hall closet.

"Where are you going?" she asked, her tone much sharper than she had intended.

"Out! I'm sick of your constant nagging, so don't bother to wait up for me."

She wanted to protest that they were not done talking, that they needed to figure out a plan, but she knew it would do no good. Scott wasn't willing to listen to her, and it was clear that in his current frame of mind, there would be no helpful solutions coming from him. So she remained silent once again.

How did it come to this? she wondered as her husband of eight years stormed out of the apartment, slamming the front door shut behind him.

VISIT HERE To Read More!

https://www.ticahousepublishing.com/amish-miller.html

Thank you for Reading

If you **love Amish Romance**, <u>Visit Here:</u>

https://amish.subscribemenow.com/

to find out about all <u>**New Hannah Miller Amish Romance Releases!**</u> **We will let you know as soon as they become available!**

If you enjoyed ***The Christmas Snowshoes,*** would you kindly take a couple minutes to leave a positive review on Amazon? It only takes a moment, and positive reviews truly make a difference. I would be so grateful! Thank you!

Turn the page to discover more Hannah Miller Amish Romances just for you!

More Amish Romance from Hannah Miller

Visit HERE for Hannah Miller's Amish Romance

https://ticahousepublishing.com/amish-miller.html

About the Author

Hannah Miller has been writing Amish Romance for the past seven years. Long intrigued by the Amish way of life, Hannah has traveled the United States, visiting different Amish communities. She treasures her Amish friends and enjoys visiting with them. Hannah makes her home in Indiana, along with her husband, Robert. Together, they have three children and seven grandchildren. Hannah loves to ride bikes in the sunshine. And if it's warm enough for a picnic, you'll find her under the nearest tree!